Cheeky Monkey's
Treasure Hunt

by Anne Cassidy

Illustrated by Lisa Smith

FRANKLIN WATTS
LONDON•SYDNEY

First published in 2010 by
Franklin Watts
338 Euston Road
London
NW1 3BH

Franklin Watts Australia
Level 17/207 Kent Street
Sydney
NSW 2000

A CIP catalogue record for this book is available
from the British Library.

ISBN 978 0 7496 9455 5 (hbk)
ISBN 978 0 7496 9465 4 (pbk)

Series Editor: Jackie Hamley
Series Advisor: Catherine Glavina
Series Designer: Peter Scoulding

Printed in China

Franklin Watts is a divison of
Hachette Children's Books,
an Hachette UK company.
www.hachette.co.uk

Wendy was going on
a treasure hunt.

She had a treasure map
and all the tools.

Then a monkey came along!

The monkey took the tools.

And the water.

And the food.

They walked through the woods.

They jumped over the stream.

They climbed up the hill.

Wendy found the big rock.

She walked ten steps.

Wendy found the tree
with no leaves.

She looked

at the ground.

The monkey dug a hole.

Wendy sat on a rock.

The monkey's spade
hit a box.

He lifted it up.

It was the treasure chest!

Wendy and the monkey
looked at the treasure.

There was a crown.
There were gold coins,
rings and necklaces.

Then the monkey picked
up the treasure chest.
He ran away!

Wendy was very angry. "Come back with my treasure, you cheeky monkey!" she shouted.

But the monkey ran on.

He raced down the hill.

He jumped over the stream.
"Come back here!"
shouted Wendy.

The monkey ran into
the woods.

He rushed through
the trees.

He got home. He opened the treasure chest ...

... but it was empty!

Wendy had all
the treasure!

Puzzle 1

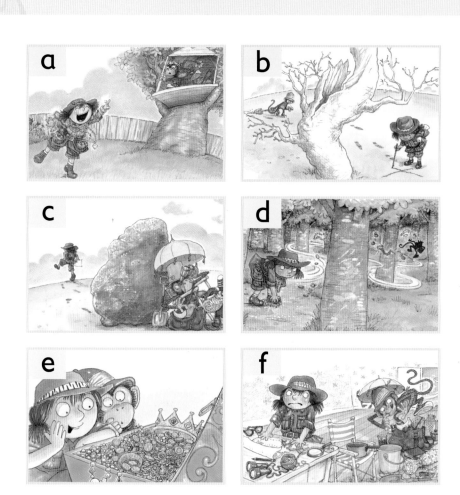

Put these pictures in the correct order.
Now tell the story in your own words.
How short can you make the story?

Puzzle 2

furious   angry

calm

shy   naughty

nervous

Choose the words which best describe each character. Can you think of any more? Pretend to be one of the characters!

Answers

Puzzle 1

The correct order is:

1f, 2c, 3b, 4e, 5d, 6a

Puzzle 2

Wendy The correct words are angry, furious.
The incorrect word is calm.

Monkey The correct word is naughty.
The incorrect words are nervous, shy.

Look out for more Leapfrog stories:

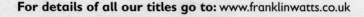

For details of all our titles go to: www.franklinwatts.co.uk

*hardback